The Big Duck

Written by
Anne Adeney

Illustrated by
Anni Axworthy

Practising CVC words plus phonemes
of more than one letter + and / the / to / no

First published in 2009 by
Franklin Watts
338 Euston Road
London NW1 3BH

Franklin Watts Australia
Hachette Children's Books
Level 17/207 Kent Street
Sydney NSW 2000

Text © Anne Adeney 2009
Illustration © Anni Axworthy 2009

A CIP catalogue record for this book is available
from the British Library.

ISBN: 978 0 7496 9152 3 (hbk)
ISBN: 978 0 7496 9161 5 (pbk)

Series Editor: Jackie Hamley
Series Advisors: Dr Barrie Wade, Dr Hilary Minns
Series Designer: Peter Scoulding

Printed in China

Franklin Watts is a division of
Hachette Children's Books,
an Hachette UK company
www.hachette.co.uk

Merci Nicoletta et la
Ferme de Beaumont
– A. Axworthy

Th ... ok.
He ... ater!

duck luck, suck, tuck
Dad bad, had, pad
pig big, dig, fig

Dad has lots of
ducks and pigs.

Dad tells Bess to
pick a duck to sell.

5

Bess picks a big duck.

7

Bess runs to get it.

The duck runs off.

It runs to the pig pen.

Bess runs and runs.

Bess gets to the duck.

13

"Hiss! Hiss!"

14

15

Bess tips back
in the mud.

16

Dad picks Bess up.

19

"It is *not* a duck!"
Dad tells Bess.

21

Puzzle Time!

Match the words that rhyme
to the pictures!

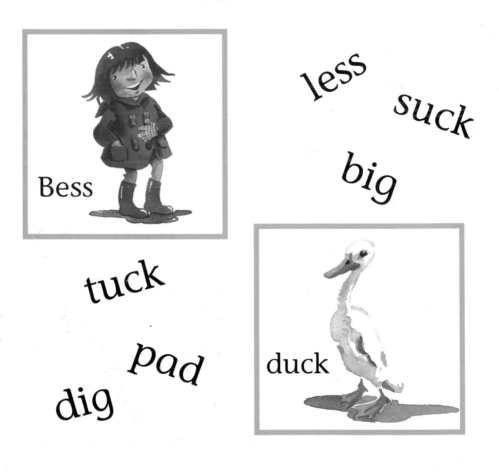

Bess

less

suck

big

tuck

pad

dig

duck

luck

mess

Dad

had

Tess

pig

fig

bad

See page 2 for answers!

Notes for parents and teachers

READING CORNER PHONICS has been structured to provide maximum support for children learning to read through synthetic phonics. The stories are designed for independent reading but may also be used by adults for sharing with young children.

The teaching of early reading through synthetic phonics focuses on the 44 sounds in the English language, and how these sounds correspond to their written form in the 26 letters of the alphabet. Carefully controlled vocabulary makes these books accessible for children at different stages of phonics teaching, progressing from simple CVC (consonant-vowel-consonant) words such as "top" (t-o-p) to trisyllabic words such as "messenger" (mess-en-ger). READING CORNER PHONICS allows children to read words in context, and also provides visual clues and repetition to further support their reading. These books will help develop the all important confidence in the new reader, and encourage a love of reading that will last a lifetime!

If you are reading this book with a child, here are a few tips:

1. Talk about the story before you start reading. Look at the cover and the title. What might the story be about? Why might the child like it?

2. Encourage the child to reread the story, and to retell the story in their own words, using the illustrations to remind them what has happened.

3. Discuss the story and see if the child can relate it to their own experience, or perhaps compare it to another story they know.

4. Give praise! Small mistakes need not always be corrected. If a child is stuck on a word, ask them to try and sound it out and then blend it together again, or model this yourself. For example "wish" w-i-sh "wish".

READING CORNER PHONICS covers two grades of synthetic phonics teaching, with three levels at each grade. Each level has a certain number of words per story, indicated by the number of bars on the spine of the book:

GRADE 1	
50 words	CVC words with short vowel sounds
70 words	CVC words plus sounds of more than one letter
100 words	Sounds of more than one letter, simple polysyllabic words

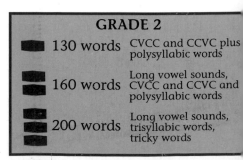

GRADE 2	
130 words	CVCC and CCVC plus polysyllabic words
160 words	Long vowel sounds, CVCC and CCVC and polysyllabic words
200 words	Long vowel sounds, trisyllabic words, tricky words